SLOTH + SPIDER
TRY DID IT ALL

WRITTEN BY
NATE MERCURO + ANDREW NTZOURAS + PRESTON TREBAS
ILLUSTRATED BY
KHAFIED M. DIHARJA

THIS BOOK, ITS MESSAGE, AND EFFORTS ARE DEDICATED TO

MADISON, ANDREW, ELLIE, LILY, AND ALL THOSE THAT DARE TO **_TRY_**

"A DIVING COMPETITION!
A DIVING COMPETITION!"

RANG THROUGH THE
TREES.
THE ANIMALS OF THE JUNGLE ALL GATHERED TO
SEE.

"WORK HARD ON YOUR STYLE, START PRACTICE
TODAY.
MAY THE **BEST** ANIMAL WIN, NOW BE ON YOUR
WAY!"

WITH THE LION'S ANNOUNCEMENT,
SLOTH HAD JUST BARELY WOKE.
"I COULD NEVER DO THAT," HE LAZILY SPOKE.

WHILE HE NESTLED BACK INTO HIS FAVORITE SPOT,
HIS OLD BUDDY SPIDER CAME ASKING,
"WHY NOT?"

"I'M A SLOTH, SO AWKWARD AND SLOW AS CAN BE.
IT'S PROBABLY BEST IF I STAY UP IN THIS TREE."

"THE COMPETITION IS FOR ALL ANIMALS, FROM THE BIG TO THE
SMALL. WITH SOME *CREATIVITY* AND *PRACTICE*, YOU
COULD BE THE BEST OF THEM ALL."

"YOU THINK AN ODD SLOTH LIKE ME COULD.
WIN?"

"YOU COULD CERTAINLY TRY . . . LET THE PRACTICE
BEGIN.

YOU'LL NEED SOMETHING DAZZLING. I'LL BE YOUR
TRAINER. NOT JUST ANY OLD DIVE, LET'S GO FOR A
GAINER!"

WITH HIS *MINDSET* CHANGING,
NOW READY TO DIG IN,
SLOTH LOOKED TO SPIDER,

"OK, LET'S BEGIN."

SLOTH CLIMBED TO POSITION, WADDLING HIS TUSH,
HE WAS EXCITED TO TAKE PART, HE JUST NEEDED THE
PUSH.

BUT AS HE CREPT TO THE EDGE WITH HIS LONG CLAWED TOES,
HE STARTED TO *SHAKE* FROM HIS FEET TO HIS NOSE.

LOOKING DOWN FROM HIS BRANCH AT THE GLISTENING POOL,
SLOTH'S DOUBT CREPT IN,
"*WILL I LOOK LIKE A* FOOL?"

THE SMILE ON SLOTH'S FACE SLOWLY TURNED TO A *FROWN*,
HE LOOKED OVER TO SPIDER, "I'M COMING BACK *DOWN*"

"BUT YOU'RE ALREADY UP THERE, YOU CAN DO THIS, MY DEAR.
SO MUCH OF LIFE'S GREATNESS IS JUST
PAST THAT FEAR."

"BUT I CAN'T. I JUST CAN'T. I'LL *FAIL*. I'LL FALL..."

"__CAN'T__ NEVER DID ANYTHING. __TRY__ DID IT ALL."

"OK, OK, I'LL *GIVE IT A GO.*
YOU CERTAINLY HAVE A WAY WITH WORDS,
YOU KNOW."

APPROACHING THE TREE'S RATHER SPRINGY LIMB,
SLOTH *TOOK A DEEP BREATH* AS DAYLIGHT
STARTED TO DIM.

BRAVELY SLOTH LEAPT AND SPUN IN THE AIR.
BUT BEFORE HE COULD FINISH, THE WATER WAS THERE.

SLOTH FLOPPED ON HIS BELLY
AND WATER RUSHED TO THE SHORE.
SMILING, HE THOUGHT, "I'VE GOT TO
<u>TRY,</u>
JUST ONCE MORE."

SPIDER WATCHED SLOTH WALK BACK TO THE
TREE,
WITH A SMILE SO BRIGHT, IT WAS ALL HE COULD
SEE.

FROM SUNUP TO SUNDOWN,
THE WORDS ECHOED IN HIS
MIND,

"THROUGH *TRYING* AND *TRYING*. SUCCESS YOU
WILL FIND."

THE COMPETITION ARRIVED, IT WAS FINALLY HERE,
SLOTH TOOK POSITION, AND FACED DOWN HIS
FEAR.

WITH ONE SPINNING MOVE, THE GAINER PERFECTED,
HE PULLED OFF A FEAT THAT
NO ONE EXPECTED.

BEAMING WITH PRIDE, SPIDER STARTED TO CRY,
GREAT THINGS CAN HAPPEN,
IF ONLY YOU
TRY.

THE END

SPECIAL THANK YOU TO
JULIE HITCHCOCK
FOR SUPPORTING AND
SPONSORING THE VISION OF
SLOTH AND SPIDER.

· The Show Matters ·

www.theshowmatters.com